This Little Tiger book belongs to:

_____

_____

_____

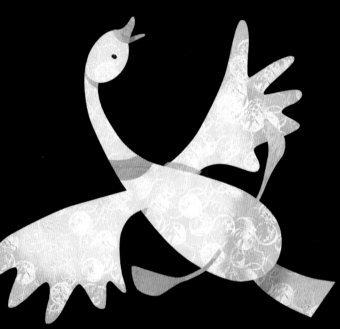

For everyone at Little Tiger,
friends and family . . .
A very BIG thank you ~ J. L.

LITTLE TIGER PRESS LTD,
an imprint of the Little Tiger Group
1 Coda Studios, 189 Munster Road, London SW6 6AW
Imported into the EEA by Penguin Random House Ireland,
Morrison Chambers, 32 Nassau Street, Dublin D02 YH68
www.littletiger.co.uk

First published in Great Britain 2016
This edition published 2020
Text and illustrations copyright © 2016 Jonny Lambert
Jonny Lambert has asserted his right to be
identified as the author and illustrator of this work
under the Copyright, Designs and Patents Act, 1988
A CIP catalogue record for this book is available
from the British Library
All rights reserved

ISBN 978-1-78881-790-5 • LTP/1800/4755/0322
Manufactured, printed, and assembled in Guangdong, China
Sixth printing, March 2022
6 8 10 9 7

by Jonny Lambert

THE GREAT
AAA-
OOo!

LITTLE TIGER

LONDON

As Mouse scampered home through the dark woods, he heard a horrible howl.

AAA-OOo!

Owl winked one beady eye.
"Hoo-hoo, was that you?"

"Not I," squeaked Mouse nervously.
"I...I...I thought it was you!"

"Not I!" hooted Owl. "If it was not you,
then who, hoo-hoo, is making this
awful AA$_A$-O$_0$$_0$?"

Bear grumbled up the tree, disturbed from
his slumber by the hullabaloo.
"Grrr!" he grizzled. "Which one of you
made that awful AA_A-O₀O?"

"Not I!" Owl huffed. "I hoot and hoot
hoo-hoo-hoo."

"Not I!" squeaked Mouse. "I scritch and scratch,
squeak and chew, but never, ever
do I AA_A-O₀O!"

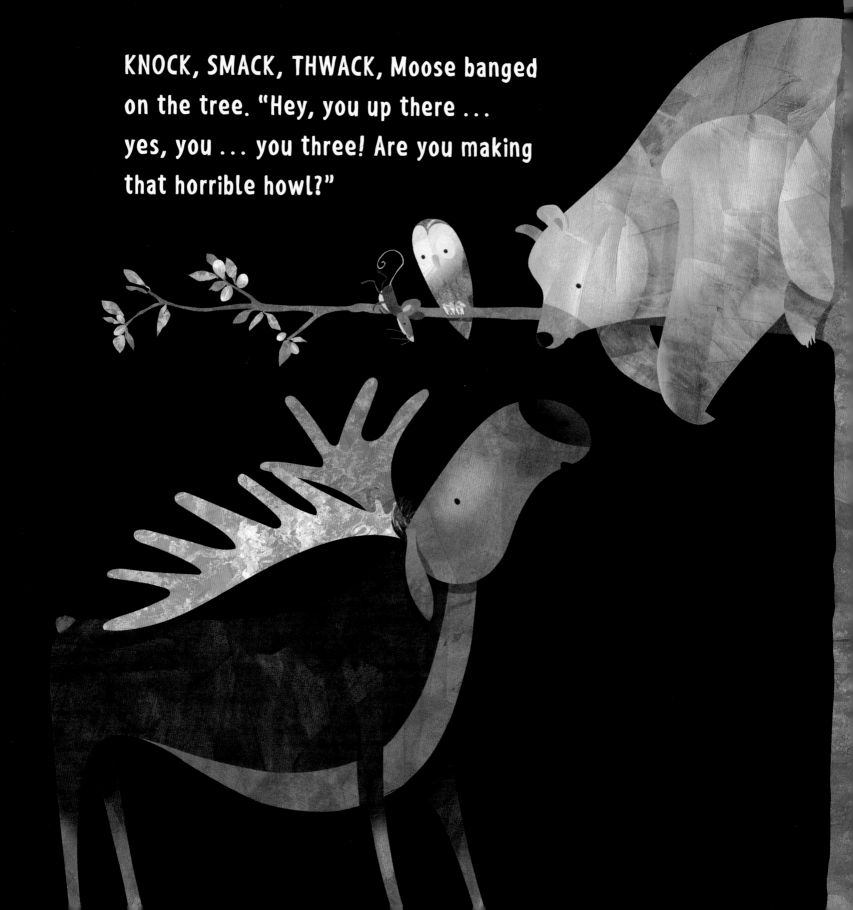

KNOCK, SMACK, THWACK, Moose banged
on the tree. "Hey, you up there ...
yes, you ... you three! Are you making
that horrible howl?"

"Not us," grunted Bear. "We growl, squeak, and hoo-hoo, but never, ever do we AA𝗔-O𝗼o!"

"Then WHO?" bellowed Moose. "WHO?" Closer and closer came the awful ...

A𝗔𝗔-O𝗼o!

A𝗔𝗔-O𝗼o!

A𝗔𝗔-O𝗼o!

"It might be a monster," squeaked
  Mouse, "bug-eyed and blue . . ."
"Or hairy and scary," cried Moose,
"with big claws—"
"And huge teeth,"
  added Bear, "that chomp,
  gnash, and chew!"

"Oh, what a mess!" hooted Owl.
"A monster in our woods?
  This will not do!"

AAA-
OOo!

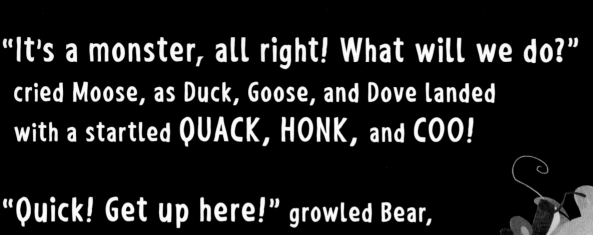

"It's a monster, all right! What will we do?"
cried Moose, as Duck, Goose, and Dove landed
with a startled QUACK, HONK, and COO!

"Quick! Get up here!" growled Bear,
scooping Wolf Cub from the ground.
"Something scary is coming, and it's
making a horrible sound!"

"Do monsters eat cubs?"
whimpered Wolf.

"Monsters eat everything!"
said Duck with a cry.

"We'll be plucked, stuffed, and roasted, and put in a pie!"

"A pie?" roared Bear.

"Save yourselves!
Follow me!"

And the animals scrambled and
clambered higher into the tree.

The animals came crashing to the ground with a

HONK!

BELLOW!

HOOT!

COO!

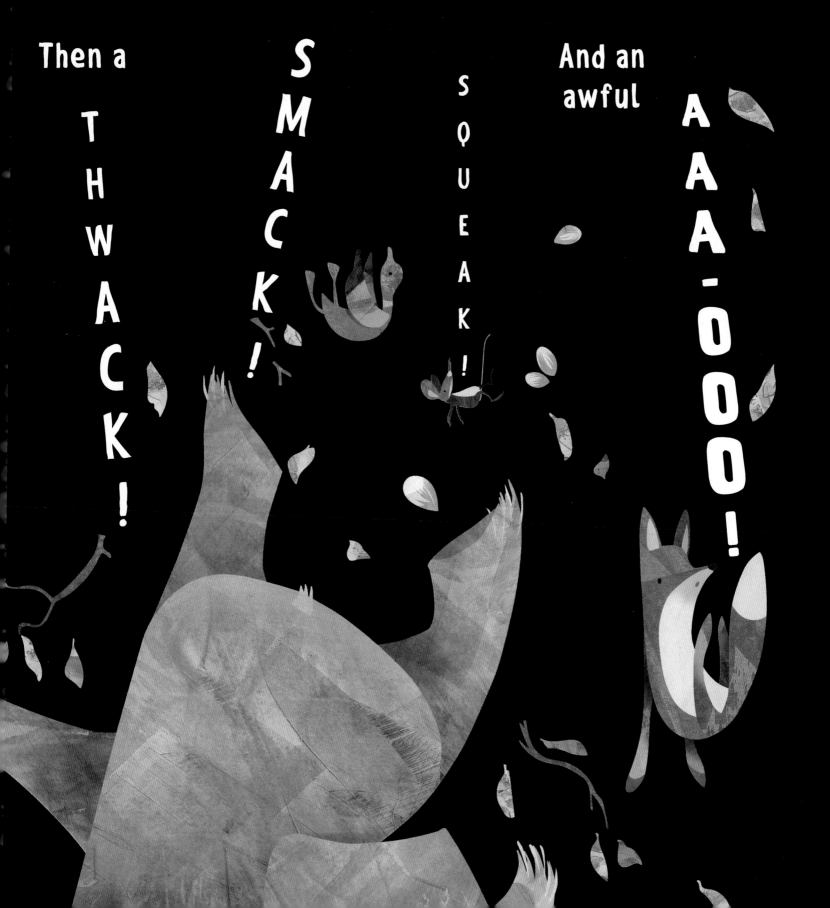

"WOLF!
It was you!" hooted Owl.
"You who made that horrible howl!"

"I'm sorry," whined Wolf.
"I didn't mean to give you
a fright. But when I'm alone
in the dark, lonely woods,
it's really **SCARY** at night."

Bear gave Wolf Cub a **huge** hug.

"There, there … it's all right.
If you promise to be quiet,
you can sleep with us tonight."

At long last, the noisy woods were peaceful once

more. The animals drifted off to sleep with a . . .

SNUFFLE, WHEEZE, SNORE . . .

SPUTTER, MUTTER, GRUMBLE, COO,

MUMBLE, MURMUR . . .

cock-a-d

oodle-doo!